FINGERPICKING

CAT STEVENS

by Marcel Robinson

Order No. AM 71358
US International Standard Book Number: 0.8256.2549.1
UK International Standard Book Number: 0.7119.1505.9

Exclusive Distributors:
Music Sales Corporation
257 Park Avenue South, New York, NY 10010 USA
Music Sales Limited
8/9 Frith Street, London W1V 5TZ England
Music Sales Pty. Limited
120 Rothschild Street, Rosebery, Sydney, NSW 2018, Australia

Printed in the United States of America by
Vicks Lithograph and Printing Corporation

Amsco Publications
New York/London/Sydney

Contents

Music and Tablature Symbols

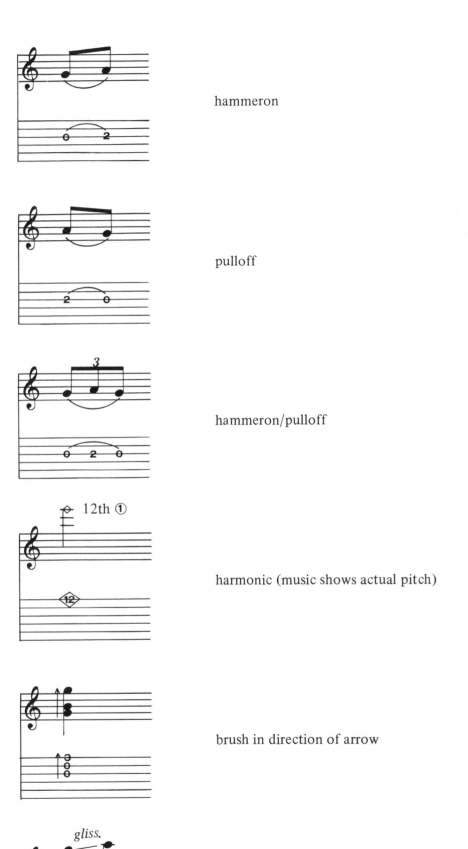

hammeron

pulloff

hammeron/pulloff

harmonic (music shows actual pitch)

brush in direction of arrow

glissando (slide)

Morning Has Broken

Musical arrangement by
Cat Stevens

6

Peace Train

Words and Music by
Cat Stevens

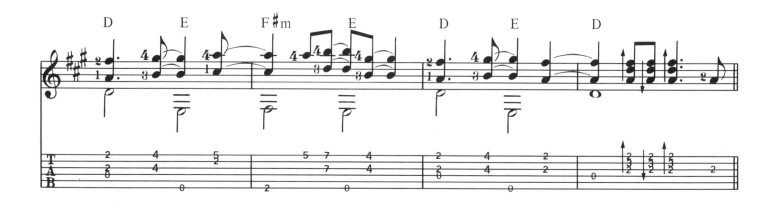

Wild World

Words and Music by
Cat Stevens

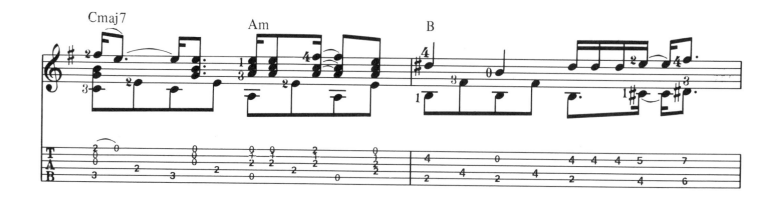

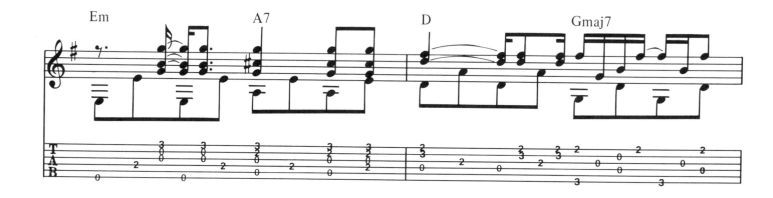

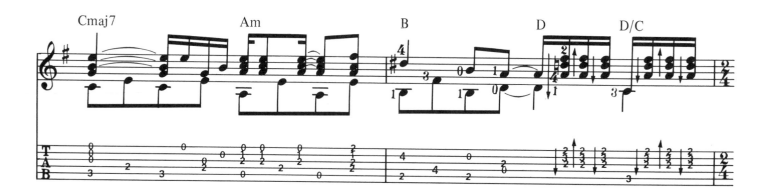

Father and Son

Words and Music by
Cat Stevens

Slowly

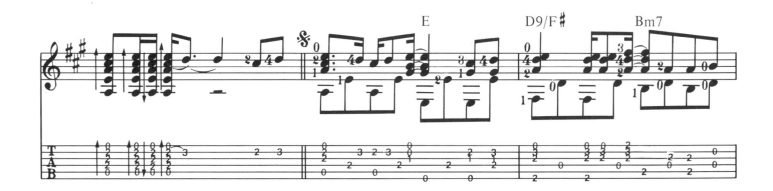

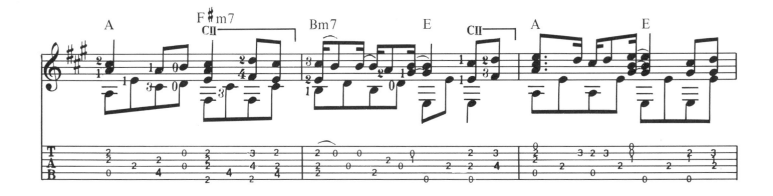

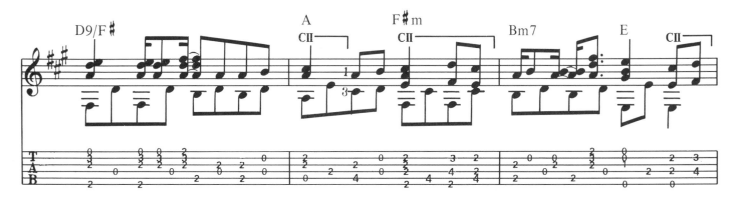

Moonshadow

Words and Music by
Cat Stevens

Oh Very Young

Moderately

Words and Music by
Cat Stevens

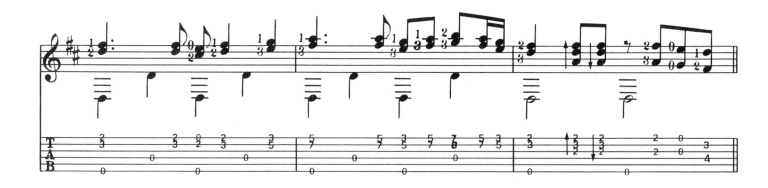

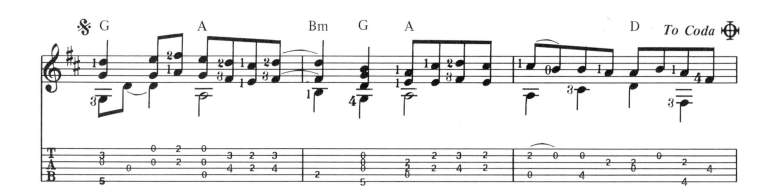

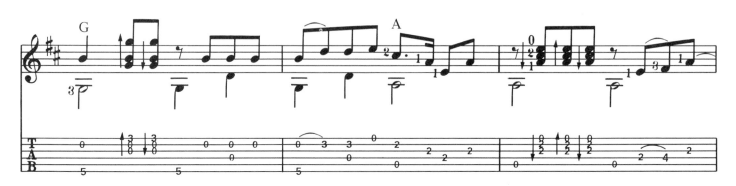

Sitting

Words and Music by
Cat Stevens

Medium, with a beat

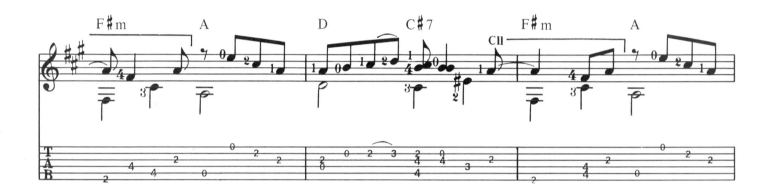

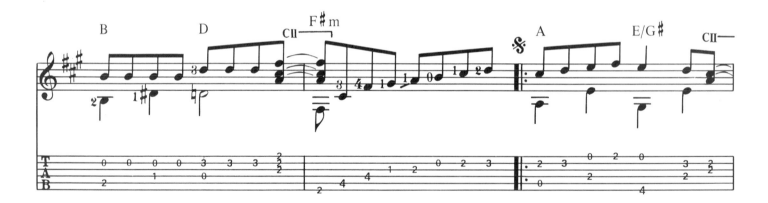

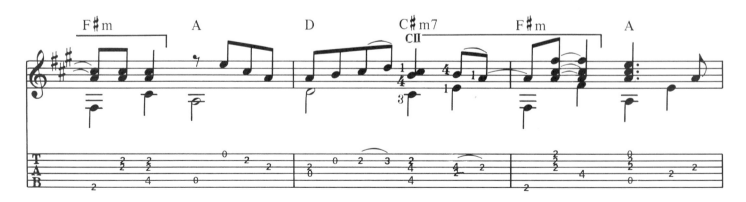

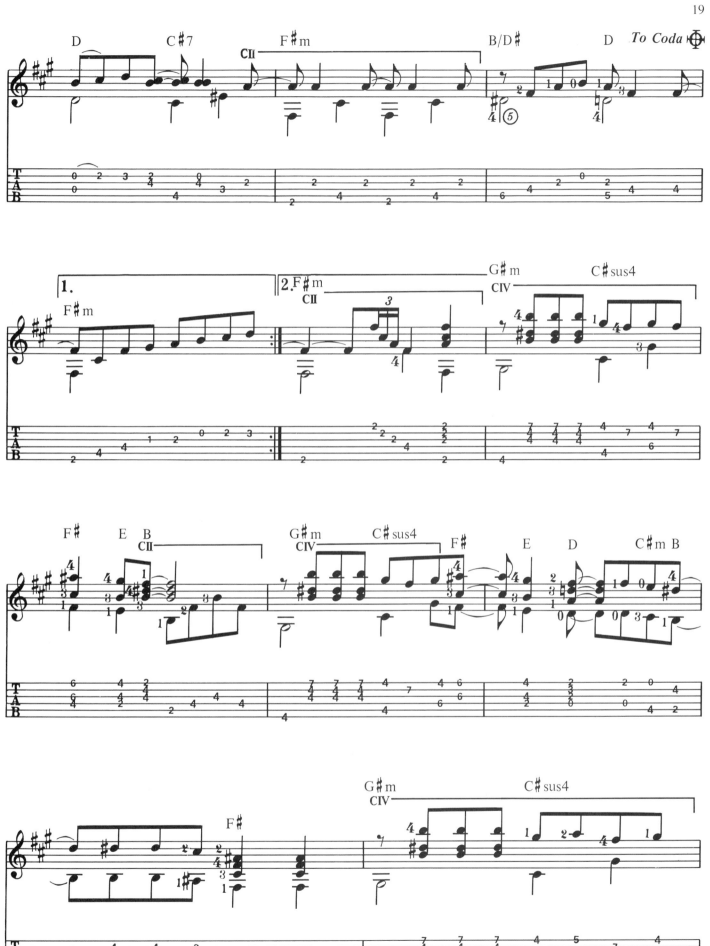

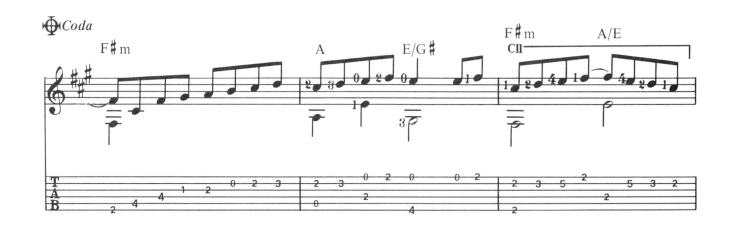

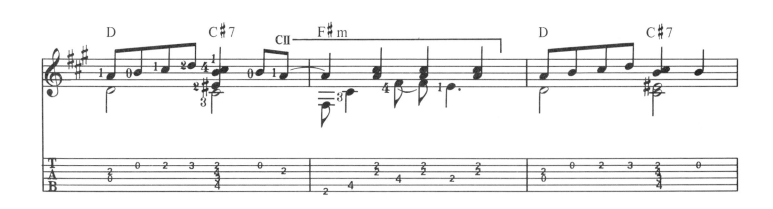

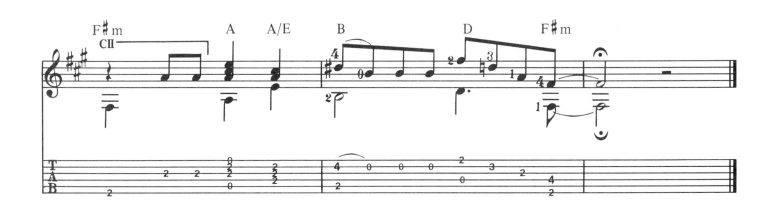

Hard Headed Woman

Words and Music by
Cat Stevens

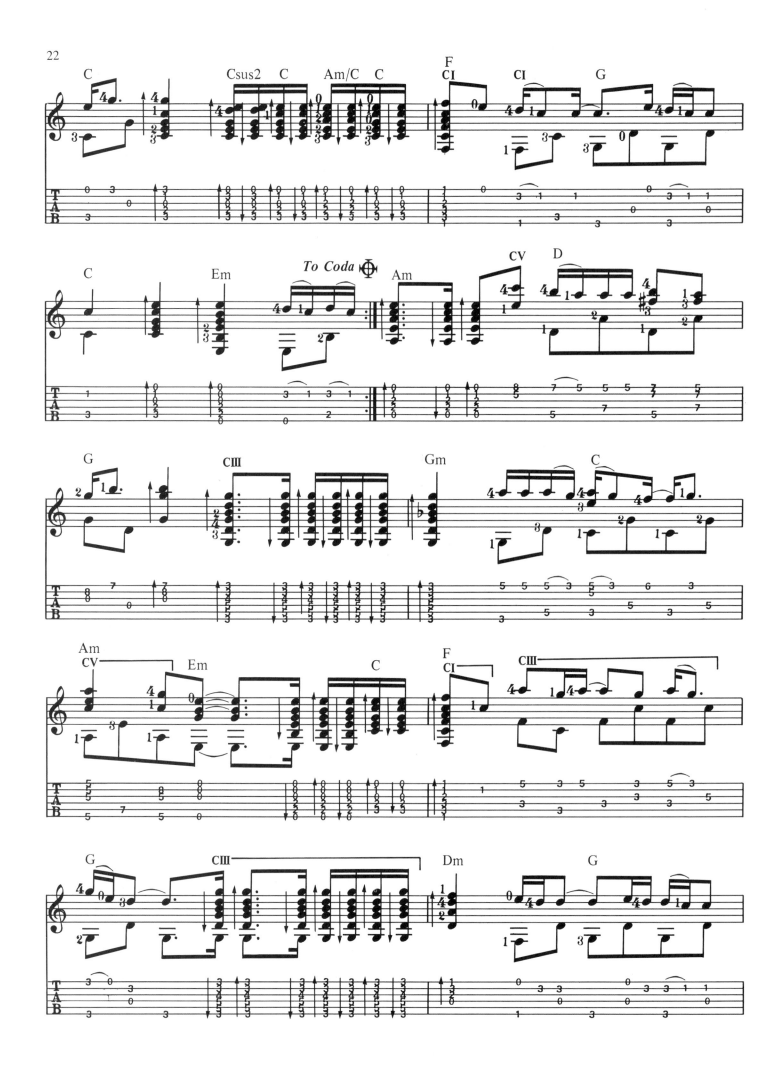

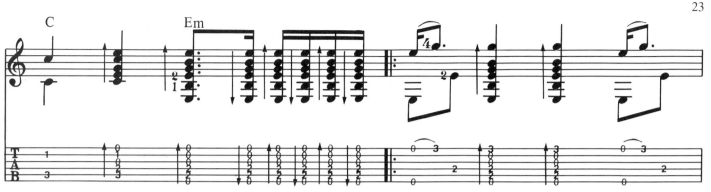

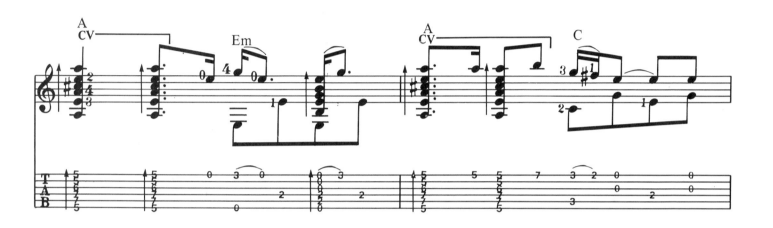

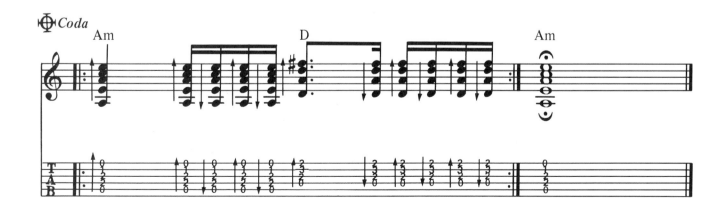

Can't Keep It In

Words and Music by
Cat Stevens

Brightly

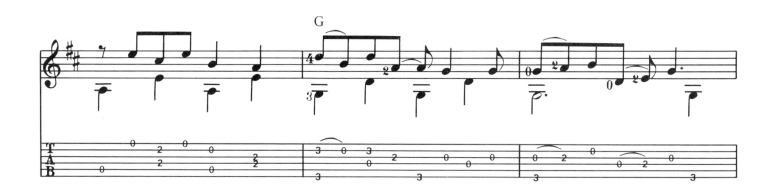

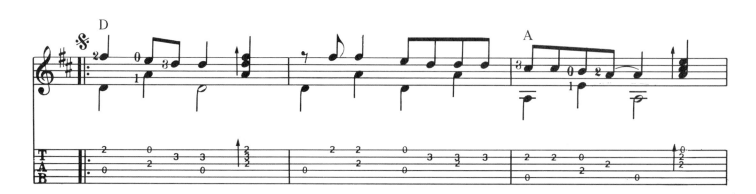

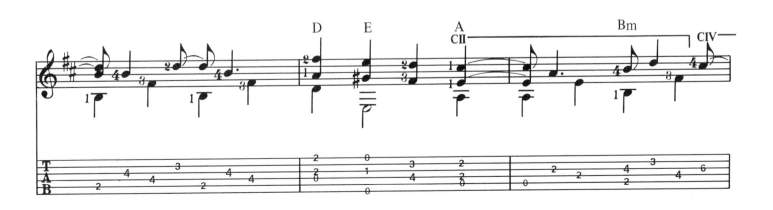

Two Fine People

Words and Music by
Cat Stevens

Where Do The Children Play?

Words and Music by
Cat Stevens

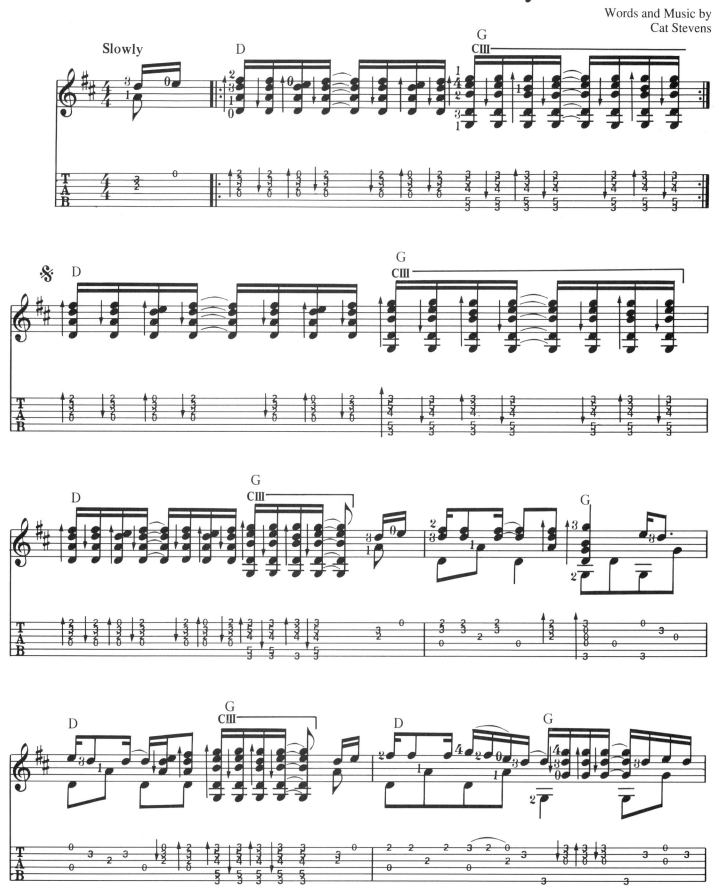

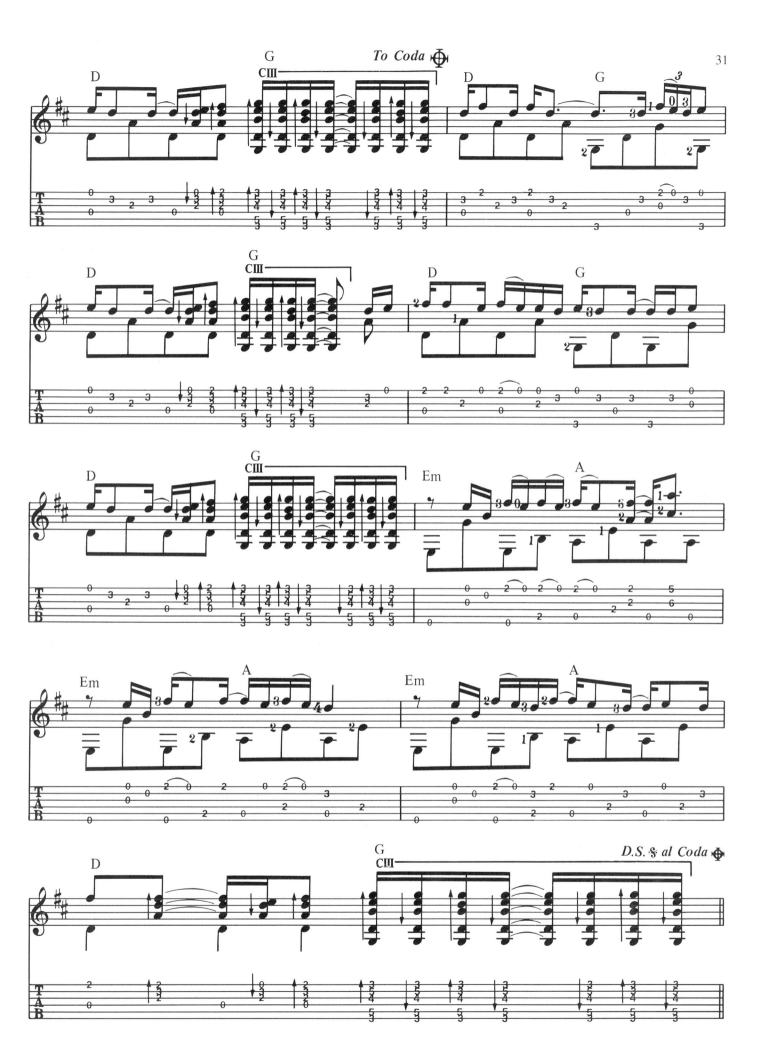

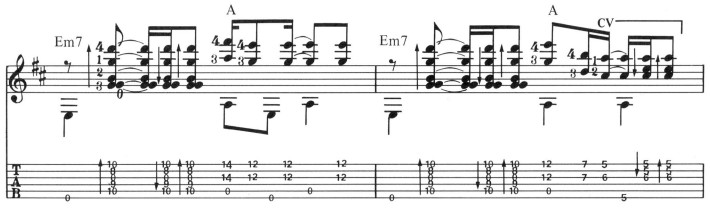

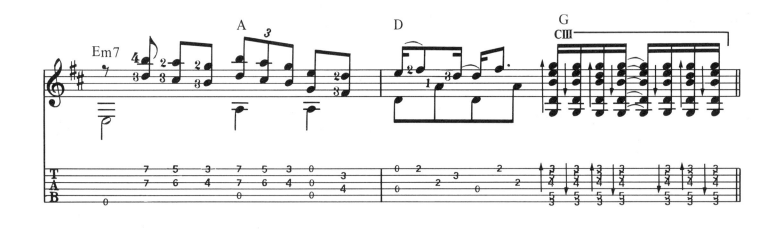

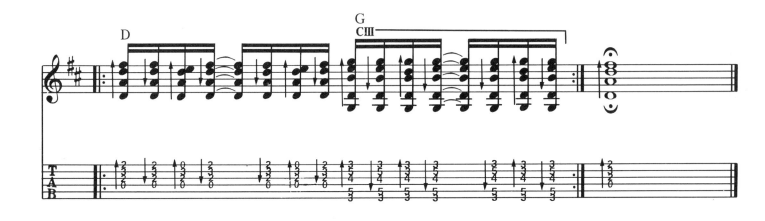

Tuesday's Dead

Words and Music by
Cat Stevens

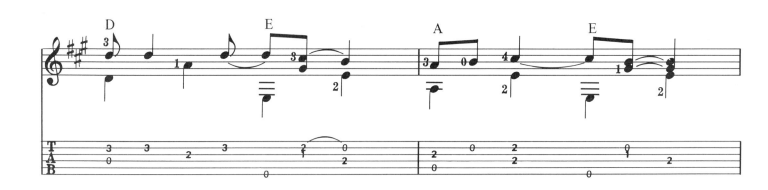

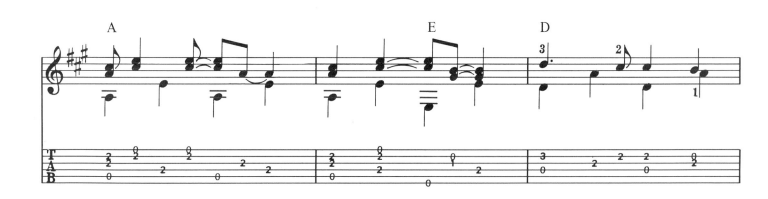

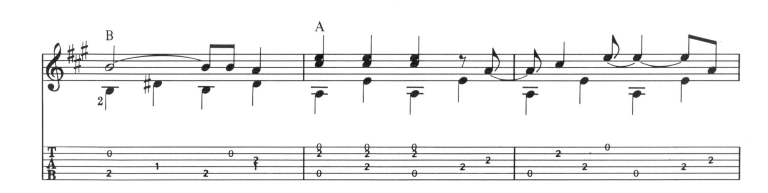

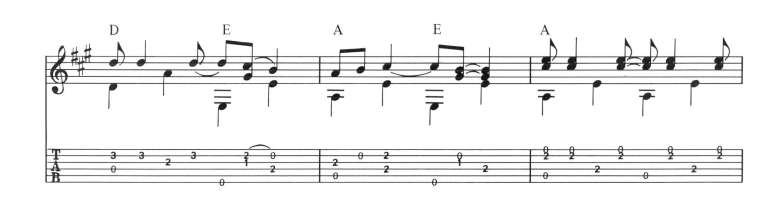

Sad Lisa

Words and Music by
Cat Stevens

The Boy With The Moon And Star On His Head

Words and Music by
Cat Stevens

Maybe You're Right

Words and Music by
Cat Stevens

But I Might Die Tonight

Words and Music by
Cat Stevens

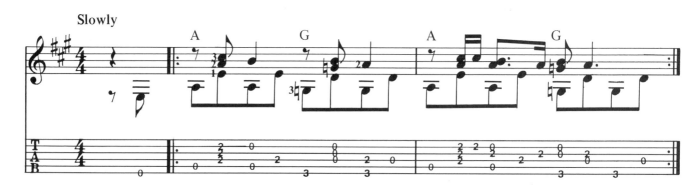

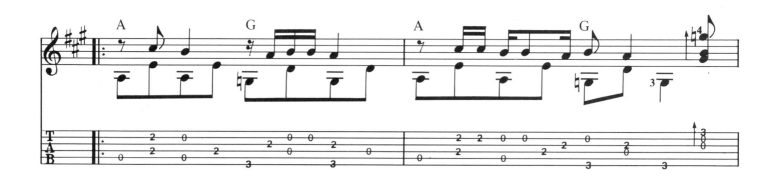

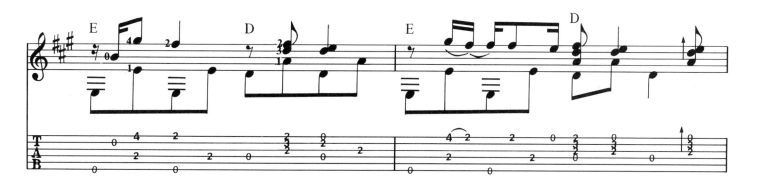

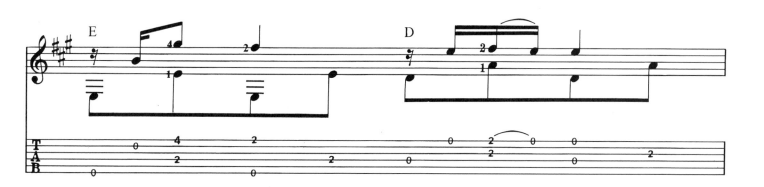

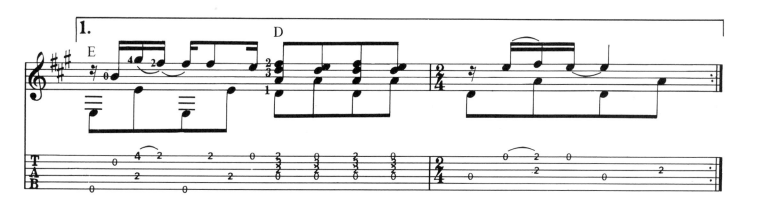